Superfast PLANES

by Mark Dubowski
Consultant: Mike Hall

BEARPORT
PUBLISHING COMPANY, INC.

New York, New York

Credits

Cover, NASA Dryden Flight Research Center Photo Collection; Title Page, NASA Dryden Flight Research Center Photo Collection; 4, NASA Dryden Flight Research Center Photo Collection; 5, Corbis; 6, USFG; 7, USFG; 8-9, USFG; 10, The Granger Collection, New York; 11, NASA Dryden Flight Research Center Photo Collection; 12, Hulton Archives/Getty Images; 13, Neil Rabinowitz/Corbis; 14, USFG; 15, NASA Dryden Flight Research Center Photo Collection; 16, Boeing; 17, Boeing; 18, NASA Dryden Flight Research Center Photo Collection; 19, NASA Dryden Flight Research Center Photo Collection; 20, NASA Dryden Flight Research Center Photo Collection; 21, TASS/Sovfoto; 22-23, Index Stock; 24, Toshihiko Sato/AP Wide World Photos; 25, AP Wide World Photos; 26, NASA Dryden Flight Research Center Photo Collection; 27, NASA Dryden Flight Research Center Photo Collection; 29, AP Wide World Photos.

Editorial development by Judy Nayer
Design & Production by Paula Jo Smith

Consultant: Mike Hall flew fighters in the United States Air Force for nearly three decades. His career began in the F-106 and ended in the F-16. Mike has flown twice the speed of sound, commanded a Fighter Wing, and was promoted to the rank of Major General.

Library of Congress Cataloging-in-Publication Data

Dubowski, Mark.
  Superfast planes / by Mark Dubowski.
     p. cm.—(Ultimate speed)
  Includes bibliographical references and index.
  ISBN 1-59716-082-2 (library binding)—ISBN 1-59716-119-5 (pbk.)
  1. Aeronautics—History—Juvenile literature. 2. Airplanes—History—Juvenile literature. I. Title. II. Series.

  TL547.D73 2006
  629.13'009—dc22

                          2005008238

For more information, write to Bearport Publishing Company, Inc., 101 Fifth Avenue, Suite 6R, New York, New York 10003. Printed in the United States of America.

1 2 3 4 5 6 7 8 9 10

CONTENTS

Ready for Takeoff

The year was 1947. The place was Muroc (MYOOR-ok) Air Base, California. A B-29 **bomber** was on the runway, ready for takeoff.

Mounted under the B-29, this X-1 was ready for launch.
The X-1 was a test plane. The "X" stands for "experimental."

The B-29 was a warplane. It was made to carry bombs. This time, however, the B-29 was carrying another airplane—the X-1.

The test pilot for this flight was Charles "Chuck" Yeager (YAY-gur). Yeager wanted to do something no one had ever done before—fly faster than the **speed of sound**. Many scientists thought such a **feat** was impossible.

The speed of sound is called Mach 1. It was named after the scientist who came up with the measurement—Ernst Mach (MAK).

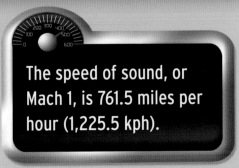

The speed of sound, or Mach 1, is 761.5 miles per hour (1,225.5 kph).

A Test in the Desert

On October 14, 1947, Chuck Yeager was about to try the impossible. Sitting behind the controls of the X-1, he was being carried higher and higher above the California desert by the B-29. Soon Yeager and his plane would be dropped into the sky. Would he be able to fly faster than the speed of sound?

The Muroc Air Base is now called Edwards Air Force Base. It is an important test site for experimental aircraft.

Aircraft testing is dangerous. Many things can go wrong. The test plane may have to land before it can get to a runway. It may even fall from the sky and crash. For these reasons, the X-1 was tested in the desert. If there was a problem, it would land far away from buildings, roads, and people.

Chuck Yeager at
Edwards Air Force Base

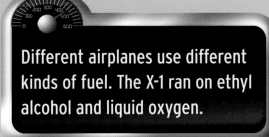

Different airplanes use different kinds of fuel. The X-1 ran on ethyl alcohol and liquid oxygen.

"Black Bertha"

The X-1 was not like other military airplanes. This plane was very small. It had thin wings and a pointed nose. Its fuselage (FYOO-suh-*lahj*), or body, was **streamlined**.

An airplane's height above sea level is called its altitude. Altitude is measured by an instrument called an altimeter.

To save the X-1's fuel for the test flight, the plane was carried to a high altitude by the B-29.

The X-1 did not carry guns or bombs. It carried only a pilot. It was built for one reason—speed.

How did this plane fly so fast? The X-1's power came from a rocket engine. This type of engine burns fuel mixed with its own oxygen supply. The pilots called the engine "Black Bertha."

The Beginning of Powered Aircraft

For thousands of years, people dreamed of flying. Many people tried to invent machines that would carry them into the sky. At last, two brothers, Wilbur and Orville Wright, came up with the answer.

The Wright brothers' plane was called the Wright Flyer. It carried one person and went only 30 miles per hour (48 kph).

The Wright brothers began by reading about the ideas of other inventors. They made and flew kites and **gliders**.

Finally, on December 17, 1903, the Wright brothers put an engine on a plane and flew the first powered aircraft. Their plane took off from the beach at Kitty Hawk, North Carolina. The flight lasted less than a minute.

Today's Boeing 747 Jumbo Jet can carry 600 passengers and fly at speeds of over 500 miles per hour (805 kph).

Planes at War

Not long after the Wright brothers invented the first powered aircraft, World War I (1914–1918) broke out in Europe. Airplanes were quickly designed to become fighter planes.

A battle between two or more planes that are flying close to each other is called a dogfight.

The first fighter planes had **propellers**. One of the fastest was the Spad 7. It flew at 130 miles per hour (209 kph). When the war was over, some fighter planes became passenger planes.

The P-51 Mustang could reach a maximum speed of about 437 mph (703 kph).

The P-51 Mustang was a famous fighter plane during World War II. Almost 15,000 were built.

Breaking the Sound Barrier

Chuck Yeager learned to fly during World War II. After the war, he was chosen to test fly the X-1 for the military.

When the B-29 finally reached 21,000 feet (6,401 m), it dropped the X-1. The small plane fell away from the **mother ship**. Yeager fired the rocket engine and the X-1 took off and climbed into the sky.

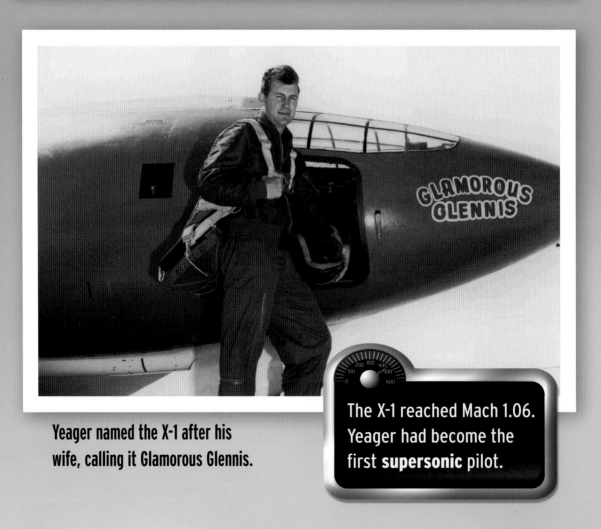

GLAMOROUS GLENNIS

Yeager named the X-1 after his wife, calling it Glamorous Glennis.

The X-1 reached Mach 1.06. Yeager had become the first **supersonic** pilot.

The plane shook as it gained speed. Yeager used the control yoke, or "steering wheel," to hold the aircraft steady.

At 41,000 feet (12,497 m), the plane broke through the **sound barrier**. Instead of spreading out, the sound waves from the airplane were squeezed together. They then made a loud noise called a "sonic boom."

A cloud sometimes forms around a plane when it breaks the sound barrier.

A New Age in Aviation

Breaking the sound barrier was the start of big changes in **aviation**. It proved that humans could go faster than the speed of sound. It led to changes in the way superfast airplanes of the future would be made. Planes would have thinner, stronger wings, designed to go fast. They would have special, high-speed **aerodynamic** bodies to cut through the wind.

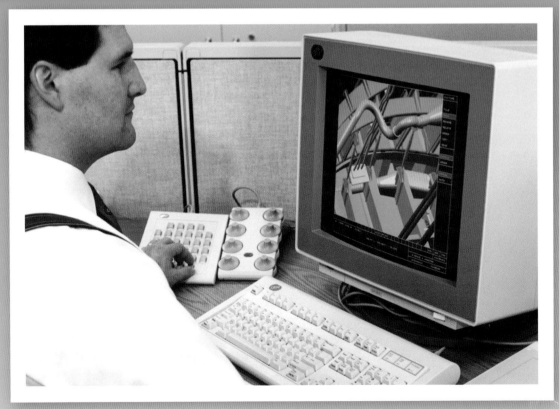

Today's airplanes are designed with the help of computers.

Yeager became a hero to many pilots. He was known for his sense of humor, too. After the first supersonic flight, he radioed, "I still got my ears on, and nothing else has fallen off, neither."

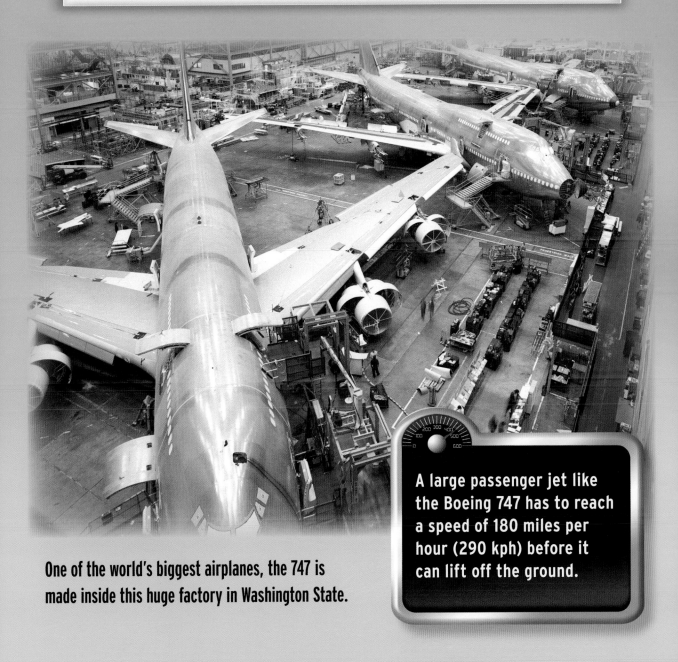

One of the world's biggest airplanes, the 747 is made inside this huge factory in Washington State.

A large passenger jet like the Boeing 747 has to reach a speed of 180 miles per hour (290 kph) before it can lift off the ground.

The SR-71 Blackbird

Engineers used what they learned from the X-1 to make faster planes. In Burbank, California, a company called Lockheed set up a top-secret laboratory just for building superfast planes. People who worked there called it the "Skunk Works." They joked that they worked so hard, they didn't even have time to take a bath.

The SR-71 made its first flight in the 1960s.

The Skunk Works became the home of the fastest military airplane ever built. Its official name was the Lockheed SR-71. It was called the "Blackbird" because of its black paint. The paint soaked up radar waves, which are used to locate airplanes.

A Blackbird can fly from New York to London in about two hours. The same trip takes about six hours in a regular plane.

The SR-71 flies so fast that it can outrun missiles.

A Plane for Spying

The Blackbird was a spy plane. It was built for the United States Air Force. Its first flight was in 1964. Its top speed was 2,100 miles per hour (3,380 kph), or Mach 3.2—more than three times the speed of sound. The Blackbird flew so fast that enemy planes could not shoot it down. Cameras on the plane took pictures of secret military bases. The information was used to prevent attacks on the United States.

When the Blackbird lands, it uses a parachute to slow down.

In the 1970s, **satellites** in outer space became the new "spy planes." Blackbirds were then used to study weather and other nonmilitary matters.

The Russian MiG-25 Foxbat is one of the fastest fighter planes ever built.

Airplanes that fly faster than Mach 1 are called "supersonic." Supersonic planes that reach speeds over Mach 5 are sometimes called "hypersonic."

The Amazing Concorde

Until 1976, supersonic planes were only used by the military. In that year, a new kind of passenger plane took off from Charles de Gaulle (di GAWL) Airport in Paris, France. It was called the Concorde (KAHN-kord).

Only 16 Concorde planes were ever built.

The Concorde flew at about Mach 2, or twice the speed of sound.

The Concorde flew at an altitude of up to 60,000 feet (18,288 m). It cruised at 1,350 miles per hour (2,173 kph). This speed was about twice as fast as regular passenger airplanes. However, the Concorde was too expensive for the average traveler. To cross the Atlantic Ocean on a regular jet cost $500. The same trip on the Concorde cost $11,000.

Disaster!

On July 25, 2000, disaster struck. A Concorde aircraft was leaving Charles de Gaulle Airport. It was headed for New York. As the plane gathered speed for takeoff, one of its tires ran over a piece of metal that had fallen off another airplane. The metal cut the tire, and the tire exploded.

This photo was taken by a passenger through the window of another plane that was on the same runway as the Concorde.

Pieces of the tire hit the engine and started a fuel leak. This leak caused a fire. The plane took off but could not stay in the air. It crashed into a hotel. All 109 people aboard the plane were killed. Three years later, Concorde supersonics stopped flying forever.

Huge clouds of smoke could be seen for miles around the Concorde crash scene.

The Future of Flight

Chuck Yeager's supersonic flight paved the way for today's superfast planes. Some of these planes are even tested without a pilot. On November 16, 2004, a small pilotless jet became the world's fastest airplane. The X-43A hit a speed that was nearly ten times the speed of sound!

The X-43A, mounted on a Pegasus rocket, is carried in the air under the wing of a B-52 aircraft. The rocket boosts the X-43A to flight speed before it lets go.

Experiments with the X-43A will help engineers learn how to make better aircraft for travel to and from outer space. Where will supersonic aviation go next? No one knows for sure—but the sky's the limit!

The X-43A flies at the top layer of Earth's atmosphere.

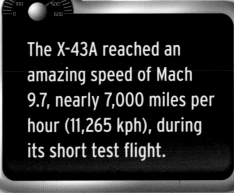

The X-43A reached an amazing speed of Mach 9.7, nearly 7,000 miles per hour (11,265 kph), during its short test flight.

- Orville and Wilbur Wright watched birds in flight to help them figure out how to build wings for the first airplane.

- In 1927, Charles Lindbergh became the first person to fly alone across the Atlantic Ocean.

- In 1932, Amelia Earhart became the first woman to cross the Atlantic Ocean alone, doing so in a record-setting 13.5 hours. Five years later, Earhart disappeared while flying over the Pacific Ocean. She and her airplane have never been found.

- American billionaire Howard R. Hughes, Jr., was considered one of the world's best pilots. In 1937, he set a new cross-country record of 7 hours, 28 minutes, 25 seconds.

- The first jets were built as fighter planes during World War II. They were much faster than planes that had propellers. The first jet in service was Germany's Messerschmitt 262, which flew at 540 miles per hour (869 kph).

TIMELINE This timeline shows some important events in the history of planes.

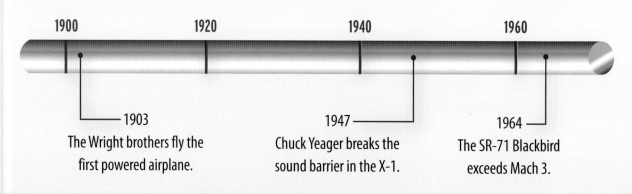

1900 — 1920 — 1940 — 1960

1903
The Wright brothers fly the first powered airplane.

1947
Chuck Yeager breaks the sound barrier in the X-1.

1964
The SR-71 Blackbird exceeds Mach 3.

- The McDonnell Douglas F-15 Eagle is one of the world's top fighter planes. It flies at 1,650 miles per hour (2,655 kph) and can climb up to 820 feet (250 m) per second.

- In 1976, Chuck Yeager received the Congressional Medal of Honor for his first supersonic flight. Then, in 1985, President Ronald Regan awarded him the Presidential Medal of Freedom. On October 14, 1997, the 50th anniversary of his first Mach 1 flight, Yeager broke the sound barrier once again. He flew in an F-15. It was his last official flight in an Air Force plane.

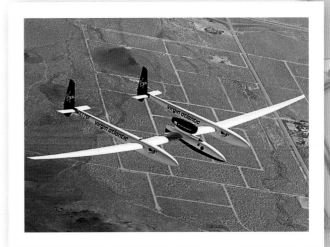

Steve Fossett test-flies his plane

- On March 3, 2005, adventurer Steve Fossett became the first person to fly solo around the world without stopping or refueling. He completed the 23,000-mile (37,015-km) journey in 67 hours.

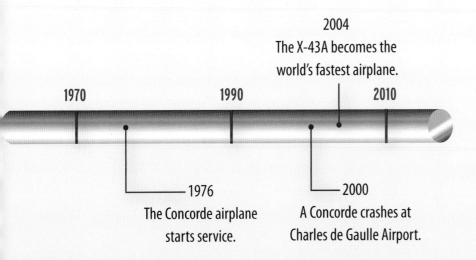

1970   1990   2010

2004
The X-43A becomes the world's fastest airplane.

1976
The Concorde airplane starts service.

2000
A Concorde crashes at Charles de Gaulle Airport.

GLOSSARY

aerodynamic (*air*-oh-dye-NAM-ik) designed to move through the air quickly and easily

aviation (*ay*-vee-AY-shuhn) the science of building and flying aircraft

bomber (BOM-ur) a warplane that drops bombs on enemy targets

engineers (en-juh-NIHRZ) people who are trained to design and build machines, such as airplanes

feat (FEET) an act or achievement that takes courage, skill, or strength

gliders (GLYE-durz) light aircraft that fly without engine power

mother ship (MUTH-ur SHIP) a large aircraft or spacecraft that carries or launches a smaller craft

propellers (pruh-PEL-urz) spinning blades at the front of an airplane that provide force to push, or propel, the plane through the air

satellites (SAT-uh-*lites*) spacecrafts that are sent into outer space to gather and send back information

sound barrier (SOWND BA-ree-ur) the idea that planes could not travel faster than the speed of sound

speed of sound (SPEED UHV SOWND) the speed at which sound waves travel through the air—about 761.5 miles per hour (1,225.5 kph)

streamlined (STREEM-*lined*) designed and shaped to move through the air quickly and easily

supersonic (soo-pur-SON-ik) a speed that is faster than the speed of sound

BIBLIOGRAPHY

www.chuckyeager.com

www.nasa.gov

www.nasm.si.edu

READ MORE

Berger, Melvin, and Gilda Berger. *How Do Airplanes Fly?* Nashville, TN: Ideals Publications (2001).

Blackburn, Ken, and Jeff Lammers. *Kids' Paper Airplane Book.* New York: Workman Publishing Company (1996).

Carson, Mary Kay. *The Wright Brothers for Kids: How They Invented the Airplane.* Chicago, IL: Chicago Review Press (2003).

Evans, Frank. *All Aboard Airplanes.* New York: Grosset & Dunlap (1994).

Graham, Ian. *Aircraft: Built for Speed.* Austin, TX: Raintree Steck-Vaughn Publishers (1998).

LEARN MORE ONLINE

Visit these Web sites to learn more about airplanes:

www.ameliaearhart.com/home.php

www.efieldtrips.org/WrightBrothers

www.42explore.com/flight.htm

INDEX

ABOUT THE AUTHOR

Mark Dubowski has written many books for young readers. He remembers, as a boy, riding his bicycle to Lambert Airport near his home in St. Louis to watch the planes take off and land, and to listen for the sonic booms. He lives in North Carolina, a few hours from Kitty Hawk, where he occasionally pilots a hang glider.